THE BED HIERARCHY

LAUREN CONNOLLY

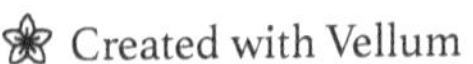 Created with Vellum

MONDAY

THIS WILL BE the final page in a chapter of my life.

Her chapter.

It was rude of her, to only make one appearance in the beginning. But things will tie off to a nice end when I see her this time. This infatuation will cease, and my life will move on.

I pull into the driveway of a house painted an odd shade of purple. The lilac fits in though, one in a line of colorful houses stretching along the beachfront.

Thick, salty air coats my skin as I step out of my car. Living in Raleigh, North Carolina, humidity is nothing new. But here on the coast, the ocean waves season the wind.

"Theo is here!"

Glancing up at the shout, I spot Melony Buchanan on the second floor deck, a phone to her ear, hand over the receiver. There's one more floor above her, this house towering high over the dunes. The woman waves down at me, and a second later a familiar head peaks over the top railing.

"You made it! Just in time for crabs." Tim Buchanan, a man I share too many embarrassing college memories with, grins down at me. The siblings faces are strikingly similar from this angle. Round cheeks, sharp noses, wide mouths made for smiling.

Just like their sister.

"Crabs sound great!" I shout up at him, heading for the stairs.

The heat of the day has begun to fade along with the setting sun, which takes away the excuse for my sweaty palms.

You've built her up in your memory. She's just an ordinary girl.

The pep talk doesn't help as I climb up to the first deck, where I give Melony a wave, and then the second deck, where I give Tim a hug.

"Thanks for inviting me. You sure I'm not crashing?"

"No way!" He pats my back before letting me go and heading for the sliding glass doors. "The Buchanan family vacation is open to friends. Has been since we were teenagers and mom and dad got tired of entertaining us. Come on, let me grab you a beer. How was the drive?"

A shiver runs through me as I step from ocean humidity into cool AC. With a reverse floor plan, the house boasts an open kitchen/living room combo that covers almost the entire top floor. On the far wall is another set of doors, plus a string of windows that reveal the Atlantic Ocean.

"Not bad," I murmur, my eyes trailing over the shadowy heads on the other side of the glass.

An icy bottle presses into my hand, and I glance down to see Tim handed me a wheat beer. "Thanks, man."

He points to the ocean-side doors. "Go say hi. Just need to finish up with this."

Clearly, my friend is in charge of dinner for the night. He grabs an oven mitt and proceeds to pull a tray of cornbread from the oven.

The first summer after I met Tim, our freshman year at UNC, I heard about the annual Buchanan family vacation. Every August, Mrs. and Mr. Buchanan find an interesting spot somewhere in the United States and rent a house large enough for them and their kids. They covered the cost, but their offspring got kitchen duty for the week to pay their way. I wonder if I'll get assigned a dinner. Hopefully everyone likes grilled cheeses.

After a bracing breath, I step out onto the deck and into a gathering.

Immediately, my attention strays to the woman on the porch swing.

Olive Buchanan.

She sways her seat and licks salt off the rim of her mixed drink. Mocha brown eyes meet mine, crinkling at the corners with her wide grin.

"Theo Phillips," she greets me. "You've finally jumped into our pool of sharks."

"We are not sharks!" Mrs. Buchanan announces, standing from her lounge chair and approaching me with arms wide for a hug. "Don't listen to Olive. We are a pod of friendly dolphins."

I chuckle, enjoying the tight way the woman squeezes me, like I'm a child of hers returned to the fold. She and her husband have stayed at my place in Raleigh a handful of times. Tim's dad shakes my hand, not bothering to lower his beer from his lips as he does.

I've been warned the Buchanan parents take their vacation drinking seriously, and that I should expect a week full of tipsiness.

The next few minutes involve greeting the rest of Tim's family. I give his fiancé Caroline a hug, happy that my friend finally convinced the wild redhead to spend the rest of her life with him. Melony's wife Diana and three-year-old son Mason give me a welcoming wave while Tim's lab Cooper approaches with a wagging tail and lolling tongue. After introductions, I end up leaning on the railing, sipping my beer, and listening to the family discuss the merits of beach versus mountains. Apparently, last year the vacation house was in Wyoming.

"Olive, why don't you show Theo his room? So he can get settled before dinner."

"You mean so he knows where to stumble to after you ply him with your skinny-dipping sangria?" The young woman responds, smirking when her mother only shrugs with an innocent smile.

Skinny-dipping sangria?

I don't have time to ponder what that drink might entail, because the next moment, Olive's warm, strong hand has hold of my wrist, and I'm being led inside.

"Where are you going? Dinner's almost ready!" Tim yells after us as his little sister pulls me toward a set of stairs.

"Keep your pants on. Just showing Theo our room."

Our room?

Down one level, we come to a closed door. "This has to stay shut at all times. Jezebel and Cooper don't mix."

"Jezebel?"

Instead of answering, Olive opens the door and pushes me through, revealing another flight of stairs. The ground level of the house lacks the open flow of the top floor. We walk down a short hallway, passing a bathroom, before entering a room with two beds.

"Welcome to the bottom of the bed hierarchy." Olive gestures with her half empty glass to the small space.

"The what?"

There's an open suitcase full of women's clothes on the floor and rumpled covers on the larger of the two beds.

This can't be happening.

What's the big deal? You're ending her chapter, remember? A mocking voice in my head throws the words back at me.

"The bed hierarchy," Olive explains, oblivious to my inner panic. "If you're going to attend Buchanan family vacations, you better memorize it." She sits with a bounce on the big mattress, the movement dislodging a few strands of hair from her messy bun. The dark curls brush her cheeks, framing intelligent eyes that watch me as I stand in the middle of the room. "It's undeniable that every rental has better bedrooms than others. That's why you want to reach as close as you can to the top of the hierarchy." Olive holds a hand high above her head. "Number one, Mom and Dad, a.k.a., the wallet. They're paying, they get first choice."

I sit across from her, trying not to stare at her toned, tanned legs.

Her hand drops an inch lower. "Tier two, infant. You have a newborn, you get a good room. Tier three, pregnant. Big belly, big bed." Olive pats her flat stomach and takes an over-exaggerated swallow of her alcoholic beverage.

"What comes next?" I ask, fascinated despite my apprehension.

"Next is couple with young kids. So that's where Melony, Diana, and Mason fall. Then you have couples, Tim and Caroline. Next is single with a pet." Olive tilts a thumb at herself. "Last is single. Or, at least, didn't bring a partner with them." She points to me.

"I'm single." The words are out before I consider why I felt the need to share my relationship status. "What about guests?" My last hope I'll find my way into a room without this woman sleeping feet away from me.

She snorts. "That's not a category. You fall where you fall. And you, Theo Philips, are under me."

If only.

I shake my head at the thought then flinch at a strange yowling noise.

"What was that?"

"That's Jezebel." Olive tilts her head, and I follow her gaze.

Framed in the doorway is a grey-striped cat with a snaggletooth.

"Is she winking at me?"

"Nah. She's only got one eye. She came like that, so it's not my fault." The Buchanan tilts the rest of her drink back, smacks her lips, and climbs from the bed. "Dinner time. Let's go before Tim starts whining."

I follow, giving the slightly demonic-looking cat a wide berth. Another threatening yowl follows us up the stairs.

The rest of the evening is full of delicious food, loving bickering, a borderline violent bout of charades, and bottomless cocktails that take all the adults past midnight.

And, all throughout, my attention returns to Olive.

My eyes track her movements. My ears seek out her voice. When she laughs, I find myself smiling along with her.

When everyone heads to bed, I trail behind her. After finishing in the bathroom, I return to our room to discover Olive propped in her bed, lamp lit, book perched on her folded knees.

Attempting to keep my eyes to myself, I focus on the twin bed left to me. Only, there's something sprawled across it. Or someone.

Jezebel has apparently decided she is above me on the bed hierarchy. When I reach a hand out to shoo her off, the entire room fills with her menacing growl.

Hands up, I turn to Olive. "Mind removing your cat?"

The woman uses her finger as a bookmark, then glances between the animal and me, grimacing all the while.

"Sorry. *I'm* not even brave enough to mess with her once she's claimed a sleeping spot."

"Are you serious?"

"Well, there's her claws. And fangs. And admirable commitment to lifelong vendettas. I like you, Theo. But I'm not sure you're worth it." Olive opens her book back up. "Maybe try the couch?"

I'm torn between annoyance and laughter. Be careful what you wish for and all that.

Problem is, when I climb the stairs again, pillow under my arm, I discover Mr. Buchannan passed out on the only couch long enough to accommodate me. His snores rattle the entire top floor.

"How is it that the guy on the top of the hierarchy is sleeping on the couch?" I demand of Olive when I walk back into our shared room.

Tossing her book aside, she chuckles. "Oh yeah. I forgot the bottom most tier. Snoring. Puts you below singles."

"Guess I'm taking the floor then." I eye the hardwood unenthusiastically.

A sigh draws my attention back to Olive. She scoots over, pulling back the covers.

"Come on, Mr. Bottom of the Rung. This bed is plenty big enough to share." Her hand pats the mattress.

This is ... not good.

Or is it exactly what I need?

Sleep next to Olive Buchanan. I'll wake up in the morning beside a grouchy, sleep-mussed version of her.

And then my six-year-long crush will be gone.

Right?

"Quit hovering. I'm tired. And I don't mind. I mean, it's not like it's the first time we've slept together, right?"

TUESDAY

WAKING up with a hard on is normal. Having it pressed against something warm is not.

Blinking the sleep from my eyes, I glance down and realize that while I stayed on my designated side of the bed, Olive shifted during the night. Not only that, my bed mate has slung a leg over my hips. A bare calf brushes my erection.

Fuck.

Other than her sleepy attempt to straddle me, Olive has kept the rest of her body to herself. She has her pillow in a bear hug, clutching the thing to her chest as if scared it might decide to leave her once she's unconscious.

Any hope I had that a sleep-mussed version of this woman would dampen my obsession is obliterated.

Olive is adorable. And sexy.

Her tank top is gifting me with a decent amount of side boob.

Or, more accurately, torturing me.

This isn't a cure from her. This is just showing me more of what I've missed all these years.

And the chapter continues.

Most people would think I'm mad from the way my mind has fixated on her. But when she came into my life it was like a comet crashing to Earth. She forever altered my topography.

Six years have passed, but the memories never faded.

First week of the semester junior year, Tim informed me his sister was coming to visit. Her summer break extended a few days longer than ours, and she was looking for a final rager before returning to her rigorous nursing program in Delaware.

When the young woman appeared, she was all tan skin, silky back hair, and mischievous smiles. I didn't know whether to curse at Tim for not inviting her sooner, or growl at him for not warning me to brace myself. The idiot probably didn't even realize how attractive she was.

But my friend definitely knew how fun she was. We spent the day exploring and eating barbecue. Then we spent the night finding the best parties. Tim's girlfriend at the time showed up and stole his attention, leaving me on Olive duty. Not that I minded. At one point, the two of us were on a ten-game winning streak, our duo dominating the beer pong table.

We probably would've gone longer if the cops hadn't showed up.

With Tim missing in action, I snuck Olive out of the house using a tiny bathroom window my shoulders could barely wedge through. We sprinted down side streets, navigating back to my apartment where we collapsed in the entryway, gasping and laughing.

Olive spent the night at my place after getting a text from her brother that he was safe and she should stay put. We watched reruns of *The Office* on my laptop and talked until 3 AM. Maybe it was the feeling of us being partners in crime, or the remaining buzz from cheap beers, or something as simple as Olive's disarming smile. But that night I told her things I hadn't even told Tim. Like how I wasn't the one to choose biology for my major, that my dad did because he wanted me to go on to medical school. I admitted how that future terrified me, but I couldn't see a way out of it. Our conversation echoes in my mind as I watch her sleeping face.

"How often do you talk to your dad?"

"Maybe every other week."

"How long do you talk for?"

"Half hour or so."

"An hour a month," she murmured. *Then nodded her head. "Twelve hours a year." Olive met my eyes then, her gaze no longer fogged by alcohol. "Give him that. Hell, be generous and give him a few full days of visits. But the rest of the days? The three hundred some a year you live without him around? Claim them. Do what you want with them. Because those are yours, Theo. Your hours. Your days. Your life. Not his."*

Soon after speaking those profound words, Olive dozed off, and I followed. I woke up the next morning to an empty bed and a note.

Thank you for sharing some of your hours with me. -O

She was gone. Already driving back to Delaware. Back to her real life. No doubt completely unaware of how she had changed mine.

I switched my majors, took on different classes, had the worst fight with my dad I've ever experienced over the phone. He cut me off, refused to pay for classes to earn what he referred to as a ridiculous and useless major. So I took on two jobs, giving up my free time to earn enough money to finish with a degree I actually wanted.

And sure, I might not make as much money as a video editor as I would have as a surgeon, but I also don't live in a continuous depressive state because I hate my job.

Surprisingly, my choice actually brought Tim and I closer together. A lot of the people who called themselves my friends drifted away when I couldn't go to their keggers or bar crawls. But Tim made sure to eat regularly at the restaurant where I waited tables. He'd join me for late night study sessions at the library. When money was tight, he'd swipe me into the dining hall.

Tim showed me what true friendship was. Which made the fact that I secretly fantasized about his sister awkward. For me at least. I never told him how her visit was the catalyst for the upset in my life. How I wanted to thank her for it. How I wish I had gotten the chance to wake up with her the next morning.

Would her leg have rested across my stomach like it does now?

In the way her limb had laid claim to me during the night, my hand also decided to settle on her calf. Unconsciously holding her in place.

Olive Buchanan clearly still holds sway over me. Coming here was a mistake.

Trying not to wake her, I slide out of the bed, feeling a combination of triumph and disappointment when I'm able to complete the maneuver without my hardness brushing her again.

Instead of using my time in the bathroom to give my dick what it wants, I turn on the shower, twisting only the cold nozzle. Touching myself to thoughts of Olive would be giving my brain permission to keep fantasizing about her.

I need an Olive exorcism. The best I can do is a freezing shock to my system, then a long run along the beach.

The sun shades the morning sky with vivid oranges and pinks, and I try to focus on those colors rather than the black of a certain woman's hair, and the cinnamon tint of her skin.

"Sleep well?" Tim asks from his spot beside the coffee maker when I get back to the house.

"Yeah." *Too well.*

The Buchanans don't have any kind of formal breakfast, everyone wandering out of their bedrooms at different times to scrounge through the kitchen. Even three-year-old Mason grabs himself an apple juice from the fridge while his mom pours the two of them bowls of cereal.

After scrambling myself some eggs and successfully not burning my toast, I settle at a table in the corner with my laptop.

I'm immersed in editing a client's video interview for their documentary, when there's a subtle shift in the air of the room. Without moving my head, I glance to the side and spot a shapely figure clad only in a bathing suit, reaching for a bowl on the top shelf of a cabinet.

Olive is awake.

I can't avert my eyes fast enough. The swimwear isn't even that provocative. The practical cut looks like something a life-guard might wear. But it reveals more of her body than I ever expected to see.

Less than my inappropriate fantasies hoped for, though.

Silently cursing at myself, I force my focus back to the half-edited video. But my concentration is broken a minute later when the Olive settles across the table from me.

For a few minutes, she loudly eats her cereal, staring at me while I try to ignore her.

I'm being rude in the pursuit of self-preservation. But if I thought my silence would bore her and send her away, I was naive.

With a clatter, she sets her empty bowl down on the table.

"What are you doing, Theodore Phillips?"

The use of my full name is strange enough to have me sliding off my headphones and meeting her eyes. Bad idea. Her noir gaze is easy to get lost in.

"Editing a video."

"You're working?"

I nod.

Olive sighs dramatically, leaning toward me across the

table. The move puts her cleavage on distracting display. "Do I need to define the word *vacation* for you?"

I bite the inside of my cheek, but it's not enough to fight off my smile.

Olive grins back at me. "Okay. Here's the deal. I'm going down to the beach. You have a half hour to finish up whatever you're working on and join me."

"What happens if I take longer?"

The woman stands and circles the table, coming to a stop beside me. Suddenly, I realize we're alone, the other Buchanans having wandered off.

The tangle of fingers in my hair focuses my entire attention back on Olive. She tugs on the strands, tilting my head back until we're staring at each other.

"Thirty minutes, Theo. Or else I'm coming up here, dripping wet"—

I'm glad my lap is hidden by the table so she doesn't see how rock hard I am.

—"and I will drench your laptop in salt water."

"That's cruel." My voice rasps, and I'm not sure if I'm talking about her threat against my computer, or the erotic way she's delivering said threat.

"I take self-care seriously. See you in a bit." Then, so quick I almost doubt it happened, she presses her soft lips against my forehead.

In the next moment she's across the room, rinsing her bowl in the sink, while I'm a maelstrom of lust and need.

Olive doesn't linger, grabbing a beach towel and sun glasses before disappearing down the stairs. Just as she moves out of sight, I hear her final warning.

"Countdown begins now!"

WEDNESDAY

Before the Buchanan family vacation, I've never understood the appeal of a sex dungeon.

Who wants to get tortured in the name of sexual pleasure?

But that's basically what these past couple days have been. Only, without release at the end.

Yesterday, I made it to the beach before Olive fulfilled her threat. When I dropped my folding chair next to Tim's, I glanced at the ocean just in time to watch his sister walking out of the water.

Every inch of her skin glistened. Wet hair stuck to the curves of her neck and top of her chest.

Pure, visual, torment.

As she crossed the sand toward me, or more accurately toward her family, I couldn't help staring. And I wondered how I ever deluded myself into thinking spending more time with her would cure myself of this wanting.

The rest of the day involved me making regular trips into the waves to cool down the response below my waist. The frequency was a consequence not only of Olive's almost bare body, but also the sound of her laughter, and the eager way she related stories of her work in an ER in Chicago. Olive's intelligence turned me on just as much as her generous ass did.

As the sun sank below the horizon, Melony cooked burgers on a grill in the driveway as the rest of us played cornhole and drank Mrs. Buchanan's different cocktail experiments. Eventually, my worries faded to the back of my mind. I existed in a hazy cloud of booze-induced happiness.

Until bedtime. Jezebel once again staked her claim, and Olive made the same offer with a smirk and a pat of her mattress. I gave in even easier than the first night.

This morning I woke, finding myself in painful arousal and my years-long crush half straddling me in her unconsciousness.

And just like the previous morning, I slunk out for an icy shower and muscle-exhausting run.

Not sure how much longer I'd be able to hide my dick's reaction to her teasing and playful threats, I made sure not to pull out my laptop. Instead, I walked down to the beach with Tim and Caroline before Olive even made it upstairs.

She joined us an hour later, and the delicious torture of her presence recommenced.

Eventually, I had to escape, worried I'd do something stupid like confess my obsession in front of her entire family. While she went for a quick dive in the waves, I returned to the house and borrowed a bike. As I rode for miles, cicadas sang a constant song, while the sun beat down on my shoulders, the heat of it almost unbearable.

And as I pedal back up the driveway, I realize that all the excursion did was fill me with regret.

The hours I spent avoiding Olive are ones I'll never get back.

At the end of the week, we'll go our separate ways. Another

six years might pass before I get to see her again. Maybe even longer.

My chest tightens, and I find myself jogging up the outer stairs, hoping that the setting sun means she'll be back at the house.

I'm in luck. Pulling open the sliding glass door, I spot her in the dining area with Caroline.

"What do you think?" Olive asks.

"I don't know. Can't you use any table?" The redhead responds.

Olive's finger taps against her lip as she ponders whatever the two women are discussing. Her eyes land on me, and she gives a little wave. "Come here, Theodore. I need your opinion."

No one calls me Theodore other than Olive. She doesn't even use it consistently, but I think I'm picking up on her pattern. The youngest Buchanan likes to be overly formal when she's poking fun at someone. Which is why the moment she calls her brother 'Timothy' we can all expect a round of verbal sparing.

Whatever joke I'm about to be the butt of, I don't even try to avoid. She beckons me, I come. Running away didn't work. Maybe I should stop fighting so hard and just let myself absorb the happiness of being around her.

It's worth a try.

"Yes, Oliviadore?" I respond, reaching her side.

She chokes on the next word she was about to speak, clearly thrown off by the nickname. Then I'm hit with a grin so joyful I have to stifle a groan.

This is what I get for playing along with her. More fuel for my pining.

Recovering from her surprise, the tempting woman mutes her smile and speaks in an even more formal tone. "I was just hoping to get your opinion on this table, Theodorenessa."

Gauntlet thrown.

I pick it up.

"What about the table, Oliviadorella?"

Melony comes in from the porch with her son, joining Caroline where she stands, watching our back and forth with wide eyes and delighted grin.

Olive pinches her bottom lip with her teeth as she clears her throat. Then, "I was hoping to put the championship team back together and have a beer pong tournament tonight. Do you think the dining room table will serve, Theodorenessavain?"

Good one.

Making as if I'm examining the surface, I lean down, eye level with the table top, fighting as hard as I can against laughing. "I'm not sure it'll count as an official tournament, with these dimensions so far out of regulation. But it'll have to do ..." I let my sentence trail off.

Just as she begins to raise her fist in victory, I finish.

"Oliviadorellamare."

"Oh no," Melony whispers, her voice low with mock horror as she clutches her young son against her chest. "Tim! Come quick! Olive broke your friend!"

"What did she do?" Tim asks as he climbs the stairs into the room, Cooper on his heels.

Even with his appearance, I can't wipe away my goofy grin.

"Nothing!" Olive declares. "My partner and I were just strategizing our beer pong reunion. That is, if any of you have the balls to go against us." She bumps her shoulder against mine and wags her eyebrows. "The ping pong balls, that is."

"I've got the biggest ping pong balls y'all've ever seen!" Mrs. Buchanan announces, strolling into the kitchen from her bedroom and cheersing the room with her half-empty glass of sangria. The Buchanan parents are the only ones with a bedroom on the top floor.

The literal top of the hierarchy.

"Maybe you don't want to brag about that, dear." Mr. Buchanan adds, following close behind his wife.

The entire room dissolves into laughter.

That evening, Diana takes charge of dinner, making tacos for the lot of us. After food, once Mason is tucked into bed, the tournament begins.

Six years may have passed, but neither Olive nor I have lost our skills. A big motivator for me is the enthusiastic hug I receive as a reward for every cup made. At 1 AM, Melony and Diana have been knocked out and retired to bed. Mrs. Buchanan nodded off on the couch while Mr. Buchanan watches the final round. Olive and I have two cups remaining, but a single red solo stands in front of Tim and Caroline.

"You got this babe," Tim whispers to his fiancé as she aims. An arc of her arm and the ball lands pretty in our front cup. My friend lets out a whoop, sets himself up, aims, then throws a rim shot.

Curses pour from his mouth as his sister cackles evilly beside me.

"Let's put them out of their misery." Olive steps up to the edge of the table. Everyone still awake watches with rapt attention as she lets her ball fly. There's the perfect plop of plastic against beer. She made it.

But we can't celebrate yet.

"Okay, Theo. You got this," her whispers of encouragement tickle over my spine.

What will she do if I make this cup?

Only one way to find out.

Line it up. Let it fly. Watch my best friend's face fall as he realizes he lost to his obnoxious sister.

"You beautiful man!" Olive flings her arms around my neck, pressing a smacking kiss to my cheek. I take advantage of her affection, gripping her waist and holding her against me for one brief, glorious moment.

Then I let her slide away.

Tim and Olive throw good natured barbs at each other as they clean up the cups. Mr. Buchanan scoops up his wife, carrying her to bed. Caroline and I head down the stairs, she turning off at the second floor, and me continuing on to the first.

The victory, small as it was, has adrenaline trickling through my veins.

Will Olive still be riding the high of it when she comes to bed?

Could the excitement lead somewhere when we're lying next to each other?

All fantasies are side-railed when I reach the bedroom.

Jezebel is there.

But she's not in her bed.

The obstinate cat has chosen to curl up on the windowsill, leaving the twin bed free and clear for the guy on the bottom of the hierarchy.

Damn it. I can't lose this.

I glance over my shoulder to make sure I'm alone.

"Here, kitty. Come on. Look at this cozy bed." My hand pats the soft blanket as I plead with the cat.

The only acknowledgement I get is a slow blink.

Olive will be down here any second. Desperation bleeds into my whisper. "Work with me, Jezebel. Don't you want an entire bed to yourself? Doesn't that sound better than a stupid windowsill?"

Not even a muscle twitch.

Footsteps sound on the staircase, and I see my chance to feel Olive's skin against mine slipping away.

And that's how I find myself picking up a demon animal, tossing it onto the bed and shoving my hands into my pockets a second before Olive strolls into the room. A delayed yowl of affront rumbles from the one-eyed cat as she glares at me.

"Did you try to move her again?" Olive asks while rummaging around in her suitcase.

I keep my expression innocent. "That's her bed. I know when I'm beat."

THURSDAY

In the dream we touch each other.

The scene my mind creates is more than I've ever had with Olive, but still not enough. Everything is a hazy mixture of hands and lips and tongues. There's an edge of pleasure, a precipice I balance on. And just when I'm sure I'm about to dive off the cliff—

I wake up.

Clenched teeth cage the curses I want to mutter at finding myself in the same position as the last two nights.

Hard with a perfect, oblivious woman's leg slung over my hips.

And so the torture continues.

I'm about to make the same retreat I have every morning when I catch sight of the alarm clock on the bedside table.

3:34 a.m.

Shit.

Too early to reasonable get up and start the day. Somehow, I have to find a way to fall back asleep. And so I lie still, trying to relax my mind.

In the darkness, my body is intensely aware of the woman

sprawled next to me.

My hand rests on her leg, having found the position while I slept. There's a slight prickle against my palm, as if she's gone a day or so without shaving. The texture is somehow more erotic than smooth skin.

She's real.

Yet still unreachable.

Olive's pillow must not be too far from my shoulder because an occasional puff of her warm breath teases me. There's also a slight pressure against my upper arm. Her hand must have found its way to my side of the bed while she slept.

Maybe I should have claimed my bed when the cat abandoned it. Is this almost-intimacy worth the painful knowledge that it isn't real?

A soft touch on my arm has my spine going rigid. My focus hones in upon that one inch of skin, waiting to see if I imagined the sensation.

Then, a second later, it comes again. A light stroke. A small tease of a finger trailing down my bicep.

Is she awake?

Worried I'm deluding myself in the pursuit of my secret longing, I perform my own test. Where my thumb rests on her calf, I draw a simple, yet purposeful circle.

The response is another path drawn with her finger, then a full palm cupping my shoulder.

Olive is awake.

And she's touching me.

I don't know what this means. Logically, the best thing to do is ask. But I'm suddenly terrified that if I speak a word, whatever spell we're under will break.

This is some kind of chance, and I don't want to lose it.

So I let my hands speak for me. My grip drags up her calf, pausing to massage the soft skin behind her knee.

Was that a gasp?

The breaths teasing over my skin seem to grow faster.

Then the body at my side shifts. Not away, as I feared. But closer.

A heavy toned thigh comes to rest on my hips, brushing the top of my erection. Now I'm the one gasping.

Heat builds where our bodies press together, and I can imagine the edges of her sleep shorts riding up. If the lights were on, I might see the rounded curve of her ass. Maybe the material would shift enough for me to glimpse whatever scrap of cotton covers the center of her.

Without sight, all that's left to me is touch.

Taking her move toward me as further invitation, my hand ventures the rest of the way up her leg. Just as I discover where skin and fabric meet, there's a distinct rock of hips. A demand.

Could she want this as much as I do?

Probably not as much, but I'll take what she's willing to give.

Pushing until I find elastic, I use my index finger to follow the path leading in between her legs. The material there is damp. When I press against it, I'm rewarded with another rocking of her hips.

I take my time, stroking the fabric, giving her every opportunity to push my hand away. Then, suddenly, she moves, and I feel soft mounds press into my shoulder as hands wrap around my unoccupied arm. Demanding nails dig into my skin.

This could be so many things. A beginning to something serious, or a quick fling at the beach with the closest warm body. Either way, it's still Olive, and I can't imagine giving up this chance to explore the secret parts of her.

Hooking my finger, I tug her panties to the side. Slick, wet heat tears a low groan from my throat. The first definitive sound in our quiet bedroom.

That is until I stroke the tight bundle of nerves at the top of her slit.

"Theo," she moans my name against my neck, where she's tucked her head.

Hell.

How long have I fantasized about that? About this?

In the darkness, I stroke Olive Buchanan, savoring every gasp and whimper, cataloging the shape of her body where it presses against mine, memorizing the smell of sweat and arousal.

There's movement, a tugging at the waistband of my shorts, and the next moment I'm on the verge of spending because her firm hand grasps the hard length I've tried to ignore this whole trip.

So much denied pleasure has my balls tightening.

Needing to feel this woman come apart before I lose my mind to passion, I sink one, and then two fingers into her pussy.

There's a cry followed by a wet swipe of a tongue on my neck.

With a thumb on her clit, I curl the fingers buried inside her, stroking her soft inner walls.

Before, Olive's body rocked against mine in an invitation. Under my ministrations she writhes in an uncontrolled demand. All the while her skilled hand works up and down my cock, using the drops of my precum to lubricate the motion.

"Close," she whispers before scraping her teeth along the taught muscle in my neck. The delicious pain has my hips jerking, my spine bowing off the bed.

Knowing I'm seconds away, I slip a third finger into her. She cries out, and I feel the orgasm pulse through her, the muscles inside her squeezing my hand.

The sensation is so erotic, it does me in.

"Olive," I groan her name, the longing in my voice turning the word into a confession delivered in the darkness. Pleasure spikes from the base of my spine, coursing up my dick. Wetness spurts from the tip of me, as her hand slides away.

We both lay panting, our breaths filling the small bedroom. At some point, hers slow and grow even. I sense she's fallen back to sleep, our escapade pairing with the early hour to bring on exhaustion.

Feeling my own lids grow heavy, I take a moment to pull her underwear back into place and shuck off my shirt where most of my cum landed.

Our actions and the darkness making me bold. I pull Olive against my chest.

When I wake up, I'm alone.

Memories return immediately, and my dick responds.

But my mind shuts the reaction down because there's no delicious warm body next to me.

Did she regret it?

Did she have fun, but only want to do it once?

A glance at the clock helps ease some nerves. I slept in. It's an hour later than I normally get up. Olive probably just woke up before me and wanted to start the day.

This is what I tell myself in the shower and as I walk up the stairs. But any hope I have of getting answers is dashed when I find the entire Buchanan clan gathered in the kitchen and dining area.

"Morning, man." Tim slaps me on the back as he walks by. The friendly gesture sends a spike of guilt through me. He has no idea what I was doing with his sister just a few hours ago. "Grab some eggs off the stove. I made too many."

"Thanks," I mumble.

After scooping a helping of scrambled eggs onto a plate, I slip into a seat across the table from Olive. She smiles at me over her cereal bowl.

I want to take that as a good sign. Problem is, her expression looks completely normal. It's the same sweet and saucy smile she gives me every morning.

What is she thinking?

"Well, it's been fun!" Diana announces, dropping her plate in the sink before wandering around the room to hug everyone.

"You're leaving?" I ask, surprised.

The rental goes until Saturday morning. At least, that's what I remember Tim saying.

Is today the last day? Was that my last night with Olive?

"Yeah. We've got a longer drive, and I have to be in the office tomorrow for a meeting," Melony explains, gathering up toys that Mason has scattered around the living area.

Relief filters through my chest, but it's smothered almost immediately.

"Bet you're both looking forward to having your own rooms for the last couple of nights." Mrs. Buchanan smiles as me over her mimosa, as if she didn't just punch my stomach with her words.

"Huh?" Is all I can manage.

"Olive moves up the hierarchy," Caroline explains while stirring sugar into her coffee.

I glance across the table at the youngest Buchanan, trying to keep all emotion off my face.

"My stuff is already in the basement room," Olive states before spooning cereal into her mouth.

The tightness in my chest eases a fraction.

"Don't be lazy, baby girl." Mr. Buchanan scolds his daughter. "Probably wouldn't take more than fifteen minutes to shift everything. I'm sure Theo would appreciate moving to a bigger bed."

My head ducks before the room can see how much blood pools in my cheeks. If anyone does glimpse the color change, maybe I can blame it on a sunburn. None of them know I've spent every night in the bigger bed already.

The urge to insist Olive doesn't have to move rises in my throat, but I shove it down.

Who in their right mind would opt for a twin bed in a shared room when they could have space all to themselves? No doubt what we did early this morning would be written across my face if I tried arguing.

Out of the corner of my eye, I catch Olive's head tilt. Still trying not to telegraph to the Buchanan family that I know what their baby girl sounds like when she comes, I keep my gaze on my breakfast.

"Sure. Guess I should claim the honor while I can," Olive murmurs.

There's no distinct emotion in her voice that I can discern. Not disappointment. Not relief.

She sounds ... neutral.

The next forkful of eggs I swallow is as tasteless as rubber.

———

A bed without Olive is useless.

Three nights was all it took to turn me into an addict, and now I can't sleep without the weight of her limbs on me. I want her to press me into the bed with her body.

Without her, I'm unmoored, shifting constantly. Unable to find comfort.

I came here with the hope of freeing myself, only to discover I'm even more lost than before.

"Damn it," I mutter, throwing my blankets off. Standing from the bed, I pace to the door, wondering if a midnight run on the beach might help me clear my mind. If not, maybe it'll exhaust me enough to go to sleep.

Problem is, when I step out into the hallway, I find my way blocked.

In the glow of a nightlight plugged into the wall, she stands a foot away, hair tangled over her shoulders, clothes wrinkled, eyes wide at my appearance.

"Olive? What are you doing here?"

For a moment her gaze traces over me, and I realize I'm shirtless for the first night since arriving. When we shared a room, I thought it might make her uncomfortable. But from the way she devours me with her eyes, I'm wishing I'd tried this earlier.

Instead of answering my question, Olive asks her own.

"Do you want your own room?"

"Hell no," I mutter before thinking it through.

But her wide grin keeps me from regretting my answer.

"Me neither," she admits.

Then her hand raises, displaying a small item pinched between her fingers.

A condom.

The curve of her brow is a silent question.

"Hell yes," I growl, grabbing her up with arms around her waist.

We fall onto the bed together, bouncing as our weight hits the springs. Once we settle, her stare connects with mine. We stay still like that, no words exchanged.

I know the sounds she makes when she comes. I've felt her inner walls grip my fingers.

But I've never kissed Olive Buchanan.

Six years, and I've never known how she tastes.

I dip my chin, finding her lips with mine. She doesn't need coaxing. In fact, I maintain control for a second at most. Then I'm on my back, her hot thighs bracketing my hips, her hands pressing my shoulders into the bed.

Olive dominates me. Her frenzied attack makes me hard.

She came here to fuck me, and I'm ready to get fucked.

Does this encounter mean anything more than two bodies joining together?

Maybe if she didn't sit up to pull off her top, exposing her bare breasts, I might have asked for a pause so we could talk.

But the time for conversations is done when her softness presses against my chest. This time when our mouths meet, our tongues stroke together. The taste of her is heady, and I suck on her lower lip eagerly.

She smells like sweat and sunscreen. Our bodies writhe until the last scraps of clothes get kicked off.

Every bit of my skin begs to be touched by her, but no area more than the hard length jutting from my hips. I stroke my hand over her ass, finding her core, groaning at the way my fingers slip in her arousal.

Olive breaks away and leans back. That's when I realize she's still holding the condom. Moving with hurried grace, she rips the package open and rolls the protection on me. No hesitation.

"We should've been doing this since night one," she murmurs.

We should've been doing this for years, I'm about to respond. Only, she chooses that moment to sink down onto my cock, slowly taking each inch of me.

My head turns to the side, teeth sinking into a pillow, all to stifle the guttural moan she elicits with her tight sheath. Thank god we have our own floor.

"Look at me, Theo."

When I do, it's hard not to immediately spill.

Olive is a queen, mounting me like the throne she deserves. Her posture is straight, her tits jutting out proudly, nipples tight with the command to be worshiped.

Muttering curses, I drag my hands up her body, cupping her boobs as I let my thumbs explore the mouthwatering buds. Soon, I'll suck on them. But for the moment, I'm just looking for something to hold onto, to keep me grounded, as she begins to ride me.

The woman I've fantasied about for years gazes down at me, panting breaths tensing her chest as she uses me for her pleasure.

You're using each other, I tell myself.

This is something I wanted, too. To get her out of my head. To move on with my life.

A quick fuck could do that. Get rid of the mystery.

But when Olive tugs on my shoulder, silently asking for me to take the top spot, another shift happens between us.

Now I stare down at her, listening to her whimpers, watching pleasure weighing on her eyelids, all as my hips thrust. Over and over I retreat, then fill her. But I don't feel my obsession fading.

Each moment she watches me claim her, my need only grows.

In a desperate effort to distract Olive from what she'll surely see in my eyes, I snake my hand between us, finding her clit.

"Oh!" She gasps, her legs falling wider, somehow allowing me to go deeper. Then it comes, that amazing clenching of her around me and the satisfied groan from her throat.

I'm on the edge, feeling too much, but confident I've hidden it.

Then her touch trails down my chest, and I meet her eyes as she lets out another gasping word.

"Theo."

A heavy moan, one that speaks of my surrender, accompanies my finish.

Once, twice, a third time I pump into her, trying to focus only on the bite of her nails, and the press of her body to mine.

Not on the pressure in my chest.

If I look at that too closely, let her know what she's done to me, I'm terrified the pleasure will turn to pain.

FRIDAY

THERE'S MORE than just a leg draped over my waist this morning. As the sun from the cracked curtains spills into the bedroom and pulls me from sleep, I realize there's an entire Olive wrapped around my torso.

We've kicked off the sheets at some point, the heat of our bodies pressed together all that was needed during the summer night.

A delirious haze of happiness just begins to soak my brain when the clomp of heavy footsteps sounds outside the bedroom.

"Wake your lazy ass up, Theo! I need help carrying the kayaks down to the beach."

Fighting off the aroused fog I woke up in, dread sweeps over me as I watch the next few seconds unfold as if they play out in slow motion.

The knob turns, the salt-rusted hinges creak, and as the door shoves open, my best friend steps into the room.

My limbs won't work, shock freezing them in place. Which means I lay sprawled, nude, in the bed, using his naked little sister as a blanket.

Tim's face slides to confusion then sudden, horrified realization.

The sound he makes is some strange combination of a yell and a scream, the volume of it shocking Olive awake. She rolls off of me and straight onto the floor, leaving my half-hard dick on full display. Not to mention, Tim now gets to see his sister's bare front in addition to her ass.

"My eyes!" He yells, slapping his hands over his face and swinging around toward the exit. Only, he misjudges the distance and runs straight into the doorjamb. As he moans in pain, Caroline appears in the doorway.

"Babe? I heard you scream! What—" Her question cuts off when she sees me. Face scorching red, her gaze jumps away, only to find a nude Olive struggling to sit up. "Oh god!"

"What's going on?" A new voice asks.

You've got to be fucking kidding me.

"Let me out of this hell!" Tim yells, still trying to find the exit with his eyes closed, but his way is blocked by Mrs. Buchanan.

I've just gathered enough of my wits to throw the bed sheet over Olive when a loud bark sounds from the hallway.

"Mom!" Olive shouts. "Did you let Cooper downstairs?"

The answer comes in the form of black bundle of fur weaving through legs, aiming straight for the twin bed Jezebel lounges on. With a shriek, the feline seeks an escape almost as desperately as Tim.

Not finding a clear route out, Jezebel goes up.

Up Tim that is.

Letting out terrified wails as it goes, the one-eyed cat scales the man, using every claw it has to latch onto his scalp.

Mayhem commences.

The next fifteen minutes consist of Olive chasing after her brother, trying to dislodge her pet, all while wearing nothing but a bed sheet. With only a beach towel wrapped around my waist, I follow the family upstairs, feeling useless as the drama continues.

Tim curses, Caroline fights to shove Cooper outside, Olive uses one hand to hold up her toga dress and the other to peel the cat off, and Mrs. Buchanan pours herself and her husband some OJ before adding a liberal amount of vodka to both glasses. The patriarch of the family raised an eyebrow when the parade of insanity reached the top floor, but he's been kind enough to sip his mimosa and not comment on what clearly went on between his daughter and me last night.

"There!" Olive sets Jezebel on the ground, and the cat streaks back downstairs. "Now stop flailing and sit. I need to clean your cuts." She uses a calm commanding voice that probably serves her well in the ER.

"She tried to flay me alive!" Tim wails, flopping down onto the couch.

Olive rolls her eyes at me before hitching her sheet higher and moving to the kitchen sink. As her daughter fills a bowl with soapy water, Mrs. Buchanan sidles up to me, her face slightly flushed. I wonder if the color is from the drama or her morning booze.

"We're all pretty relaxed here, but maybe you want to go put some shorts on?" The woman pats my shoulder with a kind smile.

"Uh. Yeah. Okay."

Fuck. This is not how I planned to do this.

But, to be fair, I had no plan. When Olive showed up at my door, I shut my brain off. No thoughts of consequences or the future.

I just wanted her.

After pulling on some shorts and a T-Shirt, I grab the pajama set I stripped off Olive last night and carry it up the two flights of stairs.

"Here, hold these to the cuts and keep pressure on them.

The bleeding should stop in a second." Olive is instructing Caroline when I approach. She gives me a grateful smile when I offer the clothes, taking them from my grasp and heading into the bathroom.

Which leaves me alone with her family.

Suddenly, I feel like all four sets of eyes are boring into me.

Maybe if Olive and I had talked, had figured out exactly what was going on between us, I would be able to meet their stares confidently. I could stand here and say "I'm crazy about her. I want to be with her. What you saw wasn't some fling."

But we didn't talk.

We just fucked.

And if I announce how I feel to her family, only for Olive to come out of the bathroom and brush off the experience, I'm not sure I could pretend to be okay.

So, like a coward, I run.

Literally.

"Going for a jog," I mutter, and sprint down the stairs.

———

The miles that disappear under my feet don't help. At one point I wonder if I can run all the way back to Raleigh. That thought doesn't last long.

Even if what comes next hurts, I can't give up any more moments with Olive.

When I get back to the house, most everyone seems to have made themselves scarce. Except for Tim, who lays on the couch with a washcloth over her eyes.

"Your eyes didn't actually burn," I feel the need to point out.

"It soothes me." Tim can be such a drama king when he wants. "You're not my only friend, you know?"

I flinch at his words.

Is he cutting me off?

Tim isn't my only friend either, but he is my closest. The first I call to talk about big life changes. The one I've stayed connected with no matter how many miles fell between us.

But maybe I should've seen this coming.

"I know," I say, struggling to keep the hurt from my voice.

"But you're the only one she asks about."

For a moment, I wonder if I misheard him.

Is he saying ...

"We video chat," he continues when I don't respond. "Pretty much every other week. Just to catch up. She tells me all those gruesome ER stories. I tell her about my job and what Caroline is up to." Tim sighs, sitting up and pulling the washcloth off his eyes to meet mine. Then his gaze flicks toward the ocean view, and I notice a familiar shape out on the deck. "Inevitably, in every single conversation, she'll ask *the* question."

"What question?"

My friend, which I'm pretty sure he still is, smirks. "I don't know if she thinks I'm oblivious or what. I mean, come on. Six years? But she always throws it in like it's an afterthought. Like I won't notice she's asking *again*."

"What question, Tim?" I remind myself it's not good to strangle my friends, even when I really want to.

The guy affects an overly feminine voice and mimes flipping hair over his shoulder. "And how is that buddy of yours, Theo, doing?"

Does North Carolina get earthquakes? Because I think the ground beneath my feet just shifted.

"And you, big idiot that you are, always get this super stupid doe eyed look on your face whenever I mention her. But it still took you *six years* to come on vacation with us? I practically had to arrange our trip in your backyard. Matchmaking is exhausting! Can you just go make an honest woman out of my hellion sister?" He collapses back on the couch, replacing his washcloth. "And learn to lock a fucking door!"

A grin breaks across my face, and I don't hesitate.

The glass door gives a muted swish when I push it open.

And there she is.

Olive Buchanan, woman of my dreams, rocks herself on the porch swing and flips to the next page in her novel, seemingly unaware of my return.

She asked about me. I thought I'd be lucky if she spared me a thought ever so often after our one and only meeting.

Turns out, I'm not the only one who couldn't forget that night.

"What would you say," her head pops up as I start to speak, "if I told you I'm planning on buying a plane ticket to Chicago?"

That secretive, enticing smile sneaks across her lips, and I remember the feel of them against my neck.

"Are you going to come visit me, Theodorenessavain?"

"I think I have to, Oliviadorellamare."

She sets aside her book and rises from the swing, sauntering toward me until only an inch separates us. A single finger trails down the front of my sweat-damp shirt, and despite the humid heat of the day, I shiver.

"Well then I guess I'd have to tell you my apartment is kinda small. And I only have one bed. So you better be ready to share."

Capturing her hand, I bring it to my mouth for a kiss.

"We can make that work."

ONE YEAR LATER

"Come on, Mom. *Two* pets has to bump us up above *one* kid." Olive presses her fists on the heavy wooden table, looming over Mrs. Buchanan. The older woman seems more interested in her margarita than her daughter's argument.

"You know the rules."

"Rules change! And might I add, Scoundrel only has the three legs." She waves at the pit bull lounging in a patch of sunlight by the back door. He's found one of the best spots, having a beautiful view of the expansive mountain lake this year's rental buts up against.

I crouch down to scratch behind the ears of the sweet beast Olive and I adopted together two months ago. Jezebel saunters toward us, hisses at Scoundrel, then struts away.

Their friendship is a work in progress.

"Stop whining. I'm on vacation. Theo, come distract my daughter before I make her sleep on the dock."

My fight against a chuckle fails, and I give in to the laughter as I wrap my arms around Olive's waist.

"Theo is my ally, not yours, Mom," she grumps, leaning back into my chest.

Without a conscious thought, my hand sneaks down to find hers, fingering the sapphire she let me put on her left ring finger the day before we went to the animal shelter.

My little claim. My final acceptance into the Buchanan family.

An announcement to the world that after seven years of pining, Olive Buchanan chose me.

"Top of the hierarchy, or bottom tier," I whisper in her ear. "As long as you're in the bed, I've got the best one in the house."

Sign up for my newsletter for book news and freebies! All subscribers get a FREE copy of LOVE AND THE LIBRARY.

Get my free book!

RESCUE ME PREVIEW

Read on for a sample of RESCUE ME, the first book in my Forget the Past series ...

RESCUE ME

PAIGE

One of these houses is mine. I'm just not exactly sure *which* one.

A sigh pushes out, weighty and exhausted, from deep in my chest. The sun set hours ago, back when I was still on the highway. Trying to read the tiny print on each of these mailboxes isn't easy after staring out the windshield for the past two days. My eyes practically crackle, begging me to close them.

Sleep. Just go to sleep.

"That one! I...I think."

I pull up alongside the curb, letting the heavy engine rumble on as I flip through photos on my phone. Martin sent me a picture two weeks ago, a selfie of him with a large tan house behind him that looks like the one I've stopped in front of. Unfortunately, the homes on either side of it are mirror reflections.

Normally, Martin's preference for uniformity doesn't bother be. Tonight, though, I wish he had picked a weird bungalow with daisies painted on the siding and a turquoise front door.

Just so I know, without a hint of a doubt, that I am parking in front of *my* house.

And I am definitely parking because I need to pick one of these clone homes before I drive myself mad puttering around this neighborhood all night.

As I shut down the engine, the whole car settles as if she's ready to sleep for the night.

"Enjoy your rest, Penelope," I mutter to the steering wheel.

I need a bed bad. A pounding started in my temples way before I even crossed the Louisiana/Mississippi border. The headache comes courtesy of long hours in the car paired with my hair being pulled up into a high, messy bun. I'd let the heavy mass down if I wasn't terrified of its condition. Two days' worth of greasiness has built up. I doubt removing my hairband would even do anything. The hair would likely continue sitting on top of my head, permanently reshaped.

My priorities have changed: before a bed, I need a shower. The vision of scrubbing a thick lather of shampoo into my scalp plays in my brain like a porno. I can imagine the transformation of the knotted mess into its normal smooth cascade.

"Butter on bread," my mom always says when she affectionately tugs on a strand.

Not sure I approve of being compared to a boring slice of white bread, but I take comfort in the fact that she's simply referring to my complexion and hair color rather than my personality.

When I push the car door open, the heavy New Orleans air embraces me. It is almost as warm and wet as an actual shower but nowhere near as refreshing. The humidity sits on my skin, weighing me down as I trudge up the front walk of a house that I hope is mine.

The easy solution would've been to just call Martin on Friday night when I decided to change my travel plans. That way my fiancé would be waiting out on the porch, ready to wave me down.

Instead, I chose the surprise method. I'd like to convince myself that this is a romantic gesture.

I just couldn't stay away from you for two more weeks!

In reality, my silence arises from shame. Whenever I let my thumb hover over his number, I couldn't even imagine how the conversation would go.

"Hey, honey! Guess what? I lost my job!" I whisper under my breath and pause with my foot on the bottom step leading up to the elevated porch.

Well, I guess I *could* say that.

Now that I'm here, potentially a few steps away from Martin, the words don't seem so inadequate. Depressing? Yeah sure. But I can clearly envision his face, how his blond brows will dip in the middle as he scowls. Not *at* me but *with* me. I can taste the glass of red wine he'll pour me as he rages over the unfair treatment.

That's when I realize why the need for surprise. I don't actually want to *talk* about how I got fired from my dream job. All I want is to see my anger reflected in the face of my partner. To feel connected to him in a way I haven't in a while.

With the moving plans, and Martin preparing to start his residency down here, and me trying to finish up all my large projects before going remote, we've barely talked. I can't even remember the last time I looked him in the eyes during a conversation. We usually just shout to each other from opposite rooms.

And sex? Well...it's been some time.

As I knock on the mystery door I hope is mine, I make a resolution. Whether I find Martin in this clone house or the one next door or the next street over, when I finally locate my fiancé, the first thing I'm going to do is stare deep into his eyes.

I'll hold his gaze until our connection is firmly reestablished. Then—after a shower—I'm going to jump his bones.

Light spills into the dark night from around the edges of the curtains. At least that means whoever lives here, hopefully Martin, is still awake. After the polite taps of my knock ring out, the steady pad of footsteps sound behind the door. I brace myself, ready to stare my fiancé down.

Only, Martin doesn't open the door.

A small slim woman dressed in a robe stands before me. She is adorably petite. I could practically fit her in my pocket. Her bare feet peek out from under the floor-length robe, and her long brown hair lays in a damp mass over her shoulders.

Envy spikes hard through me. Clearly, this woman has just taken a shower. My greasy strands weep in envy.

Also, her appearance makes it clear my navigation skills have failed me. I am no closer to my own glorious shower, having no idea which one of these houses Martin bought for the two of us to live in.

"Sorry. I thought this might be my house. Do you know a blond man? About so tall?" I hold my hand a few inches above my head like the sleep drunk idiot I am.

I'm ready to continue describing my fiancé out of pure desperation when I notice the woman's face. With a stranger knocking on her door at midnight, I would expect confusion or annoyance. But if I had to guess, her slack-jawed, wide-eyed stare is closer to horror.

Apparently, my need for a shower is even direr than I knew.

"I told you I'd get it..." The familiar rusty voice drifts from behind the stranger as my fiancé trots down a set of stairs visible just over her shoulder.

The showered girl shuffles back, so I have a clear view of Martin, clad in only a pair of gym shorts, his hair just as gloriously damp from a recent cleaning as the woman in front of me.

Our eyes meet. His top half stops, but his bottom half doesn't get the memo. Instead, one of his bare feet slips on the wooden step, and he lands hard on his ass, shocked gaze never leaving mine.

So, this *is* the right house.

It's just everything else in the world that is wrong.

Whatever way I might want to interpret this situation is made impossible when I flick my eyes back to the stranger, who I now realize is wearing *my* green, cotton robe. Red splotches scorch along the tops of her cheekbones, and guilty tears pool on her lashes.

Something dark and sickening rolls in my stomach, but I flash freeze it. After one last look at the boy I've loved since my senior year of high school, I turn to the girl he chose to hurt me for.

"You can keep the robe." Reaching out, I clasp the doorknob. "And the man." I wrench the door closed on the most devastating scene of my life and sprint back to my sleeping car.

Penelope revs to life, more dependable than any man could ever be.

I shift into first gear and tear down the street, not caring who I wake up. With the roar of my sweet girl's engine, I can't hear Martin shouting.

But I can see him. In my rearview mirror, he sprints down the street after me. I skid around a corner and lose sight of him.

And he loses me.

I drive in an emotional fog, unable to dislodge the frozen ball of grief in my chest. The devastation sticks to the inside of my skull, blocking my ability to think.

It's only when I almost run a red light that I realize I shouldn't be driving.

Pulling into the next parking lot, I somehow end up in the drive-through lane of a fast-food joint. Functioning on autopilot, I roll down my window when I reach the speaker.

"What do you want?" The woman asks with the complete disinterest that can only be achieved by someone employed for the night shift at a drive-through.

The question hits me hard. Acting as a chisel, it splits the ice in my chest apart.

Grief flows free.

"What do I want?" I laugh, high-pitched and manic. "Oh, I don't know. How about a job? Or a home? Maybe my dignity?"

And now I'm crying.

"Um...we serve chicken."

I've gone insane. Martin's betrayal has turned me into a raving loon who drives around New Orleans in the middle of the night scaring fast-food workers.

This isn't me. I'm not this type of weird.

"Oh. Right. Of course." Swiping away the tears blurring my vision and pulling in a few choking breaths, I attempt to read the glowing menu. "I guess a family meal then."

"Eight, twelve, or sixteen pieces?"

The cracked ice in my chest has given way to a massive aching hole.

"Better make it sixteen."

"You want it with sides?"

I'm not going to be able to manage many more of these questions without the crazy laughing/crying returning.

"Yeah, whatever sides are popular. And biscuits, please. I'm gonna need a whole lot of biscuits." A sob makes the last word come out choked.

She rattles off the total, and I pull around to the window to pay. A short woman wearing a goofy chicken hat gives me a kinder smile than I was expecting after my breakdown.

"I slipped an extra biscuit in there," she whispers while passing me the armload of fried comfort.

"Thank you," I mutter, keeping my eyes to myself and hoping I never run into this lovely woman again.

For a moment, I park and consider consuming the entire order myself.

The idea is tempting.

But I still need a shower and a bed.

Penelope's engine purrs like a comforting embrace, as I pull back out on the road. The headlights point toward my childhood home.

My parents are about to get a late-night visitor, bearing fried chicken and a broken heart.

DASH

Two weeks later.

"You smell like piss."

Cole glares at me and doesn't bother to take a step back. He invades my office with his presence and pungent scent.

"That's what happens when three different cats use you as a litter box." He crosses his arms, smirking down at me. "You saying I should take the rest of the day off to go wash my clothes?"

I snort, which is a mistake because it just drags in more of the urine smell. We both know he can't afford to take any time off. Every cent of his paycheck counts.

Which is apparently why he's in my space.

"Remember the rent's due by Friday. It'd be better if I could get your half before then."

"Yeah, yeah. I'll get it to you."

Cole is always on my case about rent. The guy gets antsy about money. I can't complain though. He's just trying to keep us on track.

Not that I'm not, but I have a few more debts to deal with than he does.

"And you might want to go help Kim out," he throws a thumb over his shoulder.

"Kim?"

"The new front desk worker. She's got an intense customer, and I don't think she's handling it well."

Crap.

The last thing I need is for our newest hire to quit during her first shift because of some random customer yelling at her. I shut off my computer screen and slide past Cole, holding my breath until I'm a good ten feet away from my roommate.

As I jog toward the front of the shelter, the sound of barking echoes through the walls to my right. A door opens and out walks Mandy, one of our regular volunteers. Her gray hair tumbles in a riot of curls, and her face has turned cherry red with exertion. The cause of her disheveled state comes in the form of a black pit bull, straining at the end of his leash. Mandy handles him like a pro, keeping a firm grip, biceps bulging, causing me to wonder if I'll be in as good of shape as her when I'm sixty.

"How's it going, Mandy?"

"Oh, you know, Bourbon here is just happy for his turn outside." The dog's nose points straight for the door that leads to the grassy area at the back of our facilities.

"Hey, Bourbon. You gonna go easy on Mandy?"

The dog disregards me until I pull a biscuit out of my pocket. I hold the treat in my fist and command him to sit. He hesitates a second before his butt hits the tile. I push the treat out between my knuckles, letting him have the biscuit while making sure he doesn't take any fingers in the process.

I nod at Mandy before continuing toward the front, glad to know we've got people showing up today. If the volunteers don't take the dogs for their walks, it falls on the staff.

Not that I mind spending time with the animals, but that, plus a shit ton of paperwork I've got to deal with, would mean a late night.

"I'm sorry, Ma'am, but I don't know what dog you're talking about," an apologetic voice sounds from around the corner.

"She's here. She has to be. This is where they told me they were taking her. Just, go look. Please. She's got the sweetest brown eyes you'd ever want, and her fur is Halloween tie-dye," a huskier yet still feminine voice responds.

Halloween tie-dye?

"I don't know what that means." The first speaker sounds uncomfortable, and when I turn the corner, I recognize the curvy redhead my manager introduced me to last week. Panic is clear in her eyes as she glances over at me. She looks ready to duck under the desk for escape.

I stifle my sigh. If someone being weird is throwing the new hire for this much of a loop, I'm not sure how long she's going to stick around. New Orleans is full of oddballs, and a bunch of them want to adopt animals.

Remembering the name Cole gave me, I approach with what I hope is a reassuring smile. "Hey, Kim. There a problem?"

When I reach the counter, the owner of the second voice comes into view, her hazel eyes flicking to mine. In their depths, I detect frustration.

Stepping up to the high counter, I use my much taller body to draw all of the customer's attention, hoping to give Kim a break so she won't flee.

The customer is a young woman, far from the most intimidating of people we've had wander in here. She tilts her chin up but doesn't have to crane her head as much as most girls do to meet my gaze. The stranger is pretty, in the classic blonde American pie kind of way. Her skin doesn't have a single freckle marking its smooth paleness, and her delicate lips sit pretty and pink under a cute nose.

Sweet. The thought pops, unbidden, into my mind.

She's the embodiment of the word. Like a pink lollipop.

A sense of familiarity spikes in the back of my brain, but I don't understand it.

There's only one crack in her perfect candy form, and that's a delicate slash through her slim eyebrow. That scar, small as it is, makes her seem more approachable. If only slightly.

"Um, this woman thinks we have her dog." Kim glances down at the computer screen, then to the flyers on the desk in front of her, then up to me, as if in one of these three places she'll find the answer to the problem.

"I don't think it. I *know* it." The woman may look sweet, but she sounds like an angry hornet stuck in a coke can.

Again, I have to suppress another sigh. Running the front desk hasn't been my job for eight months, but it looks like today I need to take the reins.

"How, exactly, do you know we have your dog? Was it removed from your care? Did you abandon it here?"

The lollipop gasps, clearly offended.

"No! I would *never* abandon her. The officer who picked her up said this is where I should come to get her."

"So, she was removed? If the court ordered—"

"No one took her from me! I'm the one who called the cops!" The young woman snaps her mouth shut, eyes going wide, clearly surprised by her outburst. Her gaze drops, and a frustrated breath ruffles a few blonde strands of hair that have come loose from her ponytail.

Kim and I share a baffled look.

"Ma'am, I don't understand—"

"I'm not a *ma'am*. Ma'ams have their shit together." She lets out a soft growl, and I try not to think about how cute the sound is. "Sorry, sorry. I'm messing this up." Her voice lowers, almost as if she's talking to herself. "Get a hold of yourself."

I don't know what to make of this woman. For some reason, I feel the urge to circle around the counter and rub a reassuring hand over her back.

Since when did I become the comforting type?

Instead, I keep my voice level and firm, the way I would with a stressed animal.

"Why don't you start at the beginning?"

The pretty customer blinks, raising her gaze enough to meet mine again. In the bright fluorescent light, I catch a hint of green just around her pupils.

"The beginning. Okay. Like a story. I can do that." She breaths in deep, as if settling herself, then starts the tale, almost rapid-fire with her words. "Yesterday, I was running. I've been doing that more lately because...well, that's not important. So, I was running. And I heard this sound. I don't wear headphones when I run. It's not safe. You should always be aware of your surroundings." She makes a wide gesture with her arms as if Kim and I are students in a self-defense class and she's the instructor. "The noise made me stop. Then I heard it again. Like a whining. It was coming from a side street, so I walked towards it. The alley was filthy. Mud everywhere. But, you know, it's New Orleans. Everything is wet all the time. And New York wasn't pristine by any means. So, dirty street, no big deal, right? Then I saw her."

The woman pauses, gaze distracted, as if she's replaying the memory, not seeing me or the shelter's waiting room anymore.

"Saw who?" Apparently, the story has Kim captivated because the redhead leans forward, voice hushed as she asks the question.

The woman blinks, coming back to us. "My dog. Well, I guess she's not technically *mine*. Yet. In a legal sense." The blonde places a piece of paper she's been clutching on the counter, smoothing it flat.

An adoption form.

"But she's mine in a *soulful* sense. I know she is. I found her. Or she found me." The customer worries her bottom lip. "She was in bad shape. Which is why I called 9-1-1. Because I didn't know what else to do. How to help her. But I know now. I want to take her home with me."

As I pick up the application, my eyes seek out the first line for some vital information.

Paige Herbert.

"Paige?"

She nods and gifts me with half a smile. The curve of those perfectly-shaped lips sends a warning shot through me. Suddenly, I realize why she seems familiar.

I doubt I've ever met this particular girl before, but I've met her type. Dealt with them all through grade school. The Paige Herberts of the world—pale, blonde, pretty—are used to getting their way. Teachers give them A's for showing up and smiling. Boys trip over themselves to carry their lunch trays. Everyone jockeys to sit next to them on the bus, and in class, and at the lunch table.

The rare times those girls took notice of me, their noses wrinkled, and their mouths sneered. They'd whispered behind their hands to friends and giggled as their mascara lashed eyes flicked my way.

When I was a kid, the spoiled rich guys did their best to break me down physically, but it was the pampered blonde girls that messed with my psyche.

As an adult, I've done a good job avoiding Paige Herbert's kind.

It's in my best interest to get things figured out and send her on her way.

"What did the dog look like?" As far as I know, three dogs were picked up yesterday. My guess is she's looking for the Pomeranian. After a bath, the thing was pretty cute, but those small dogs come with huge attitudes.

"Like I was saying. She's got these huge brown eyes that just carve out your heart. And she's this wonderful Halloween tie-dye color." The woman, Paige, stares at me with expectation, as if what she just said makes any sort of sense.

"So...pretty fluffy? About this big?" I use my hands to indicate something the size of a basketball.

Paige's light eyebrows dip down as her mouth pinches. "What? No. Her hair is short. And she's at least this tall." When she steps back from the counter, her hand hovers at mid-thigh.

I wish she hadn't done that.

Our counters are tall, about chest-high on most people, to keep dogs that get loose from jumping over them. Now that Paige stands far enough away to indicate the size of the dog, I get a full view of her body.

She's wearing those stretchy exercise clothes that cling to every curve. And hell, does she have some nice curves.

Before I can linger too long on the peaks and valleys of her luscious hips and chest, I tear my eyes away and pretend to read over her application while forcing my mind back to dogs.

The only one that came in yesterday that even remotely fits her description is a pit bull, which is not what I would've guessed. That dog was pretty beat up. Cuts and scratches littered its brindle coat...

That's when it clicks.

Brindle, aka, a combination of black and burnt orange. Halloween tie-dye.

She definitely means the pit bull.

My shoulders sag, just a bit.

"Okay, yeah. I know the dog you're talking about."

"You do?" Paige steps forward to grip the edge of the counter, excitement clear in her voice.

I don't want to have to look at her joyous smile, knowing the sight will just unsettle me, so I keep my eyes averted.

"Yeah. Pit bull. Brought in around ten in the morning. Found chained up with a duct tape muzzle. Probably used as a bait dog."

"That's her." Her response is less enthusiastic but still eager. "Can I take her home?"

With the trouble we have adopting out pit bulls, I should be overjoyed to have someone here, asking for one. Problem is, I'm not sold on Paige. She shows up to the shelter in the middle of a weekday when most people are at their full-time jobs, dressed like she's on her way to a yoga class. My guess is she's a bored housewife looking for a charity project, and I don't like the idea of her adopting a dog on a whim, only to find she can't handle the responsibility.

Luckily, I have a completely valid excuse for turning her away.

"The dog is still getting checked out by the vet. Stitching cuts is quick, but she might have infections that take longer to treat. Then after that she needs to go through different socialization and behavioral tests before we can make her available for adoption." Tired of talking to a piece of paper, but not wanting to meet her pleading eyes, I instead focus on the imperfect scar. "You're looking at anywhere from a couple weeks to a couple months."

"So then, I just come back every day to check in? Does she have an ID number assigned to her so there's no confusion in the future?" Paige tilts her head to the side just enough to catch my eye, and I find myself stumbling over a response. Her unwavering commitment to the animal is making me doubt my initial assumption, and my skeptical heart has to admit there might be a slight chance she follows through.

I'm tempted to tell her that yes, she does need to come back to the shelter every day. Partly to find out if she actually would, but also a little bit because I wouldn't mind listening to her weird rambling a few more times.

I shouldn't want to do anything with her, I remind myself.

"We can take down your name and phone number and give you a call when she's available. But there's only a twenty-four-hour hold, then she's up for anyone interested." I say that like there's real competition. The general public's fear of pit bulls means they tend to stick around longer than other breeds.

"That won't happen. You call me, I'll be here." She leans over the counter, squinting her eyes at my chest. "Dash."

I flinch in surprise, not expecting to hear my name in her husky, sweet voice. The sound puts me in a temporary daze, until I realize I'm wearing a name tag.

"Well"—I clear my throat— "we have your contact info here." I hand the application form to Kim, who's been watching the entire exchange with the fascination of a person trying to learn her new job.

Paige nods steps back, affording me another view of her full, fit body. I shove my clenched hands into my pockets and move to retreat to my office.

"Dash." The pleading tone she uses tightens my skin in a delicious way. As hazel eyes stare me down, I meet her intense gaze, knowing all the while that I shouldn't. "Tell her that I'm coming back for her. She's mine, and I'm hers. Tell her that."

The request is so odd, I can't do anything other than nod.

A hesitant smile curves at the corners of Paige Herbert's mouth before she turns abruptly, her neon green sneakers squeaking on the linoleum tiles as she strolls out of the front entrance.

Kim and I share baffled looks.

"So, does that happen a lot?" She asks.

I swallow past the blockage in my throat caused by Paige's half-smile.

"No. That...that was new."

Keep reading...

PLEASE REVIEW THIS BOOK!

Thank you for reading *The Bed Hierarchy*! I hope you enjoyed this adorable romantic comedy and that you'll check out a few more of my books.

I would also be grateful if you could take a moment to **rate and review** this book. Reviews mean the world to me. The more reviews a book has, the easier it is for other readers to find my work. Running my small writing business means every reader is important! I love you all so much!

ALSO BY LAUREN CONNOLLY

ABOUT THE AUTHOR

Lauren Connolly is a Colorado Book Awards Finalist and an author of contemporary and paranormal romance stories. As a librarian, she knows the importance of citing sources, often falling down research rabbit holes when working on her novels. Lauren can never seem to stay in one place for too long, but trust that wherever she's living there is a dog who thinks he's a troll, twin cats hiding in the couch, and bookshelves bursting with the diverse stories written by the authors she loves.